The Ruin of Beltany Ring

A Collection of Pagan Poems and Tales

C. S. MacCath

Triskele Media Press

First published in 2013 by

Triskele Media Press

South Haven, Nova Scotia B0E 1B0

First Printing, 2013

Second Printing, 2025

Cover Photograph by Joe Langan

PRINT ISBN-13: 978-1-0693038-1-3

EBOOK ISBN-13: 978-1-0693038-0-6

For Sean

Contents

Introduction

I first met C.S. MacCath when we both took part in a Pagan short story contest put on by Llewellyn Worldwide and BBI Media. The winning entries, including ours, became part of a first-ever collection called *The Pagan Anthology of Short Fiction: 13 Prize Winning Tales*. The book was filled with Pagan-centric stories of every style imaginable; contemporary, fantasy, science fiction, even a western. Some of the authors went on to become successful multi-published authors. Others, no doubt, are still stirring their cauldrons of creativity, somewhere out there.

But none of the writers I met impressed me so much as one: C.S. MacCath. Not only did I love her story, but I found the woman herself to be charming; warm and clever, witty and wise, earthy and larger-than-life. In the years that passed since that chance meeting at Pantheacon, where the awards were presented, I have followed her career with great interest.

My first impressions proved to be true, as both her real-life adventures and her writing endeavors continued to impress and amaze me. A Pagan who truly walks her talk, C.S. spends her time working for the betterment of our natural world, rescuing orphaned and injured wildlife, learning and advocating for the Scottish Gaelic language and of course, writing. Unceasingly supportive of other writers and Pagans, she walks her path with courage and conviction I have seen in few people and writes with a gift that is even rarer.

That anthology where our stories came together was intended to be the first of many. But alas, that particular dream did not come true. Sadly, there is very little out there in the way of fiction specifically written by Pagans for a Pagan audience or for those who are interested in learning more about us and catching a glimpse into our hidden ways. There are many nonfiction books on modern Witchcraft (some of which I've written), but until now, the lyrical, magical, spiritual voice of the Pagan author has gone largely unheard.

Thankfully, this collection changes all that. With C.S. MacCath's vivid poetry and evocative, sometimes heartrendingly beautiful tales, Pagan fiction finally has a shining star to guide us to new worlds and give us a clearer look at the world in which we live. And that's what I call magic.

Deborah Blake
Author of *The Goddess Is in the Details*

Fetters

We dive into the abyssal waters -
of that otherness, trancing,
archaic symbols twining -
about our throats, silvery nooses,
old soul memory a provenance -
of oxygen, nourishing our cells,
and the world is transformed.

There, behind the chemical burn -
of cubicle food,
a fall of sun-warmed apricots,
orange and sweet.
There, beneath a smooth -
mortuary of concrete,
billions of seeds, patient as suns,
wait to uncurl.
There, beyond the gabble and woe -
of a hundred channels,
a living Earth calls to us,

strains our fetters-

with a voice like the chime of a waterfall:

"WILL YOU NOT COME? Will you not leap like a stag onto the crossroads, and turn to the left, the way of removing, and turn again until your fetters are broken? Will you not flee into the forest then, and be free?"

Surfacing, our silvery symbols -
burn like frostbite,
flashing with a moon-white intensity -
we had never reckoned,
pulling us out, out, out.
We can see the road now, just there,
but our fetters are bloody razor wire,
cutting our flesh,
and between them, we weep.

Ink for the Dead

HER HANDS TREMBLE as she hands me the picture. The paper is crumpled as though it has been wadded up and smoothed a hundred times. I take it from her and try not to gaze too long at the crow's feet around her eyes and the gaunt prominence of her cheekbones. She looks as if she herself might crumple if I refuse her. Folding her hands in her lap, she stares out the window and down the street as if waiting for her long overdue strength to return from some vital errand. There are deep needle tracks in the flesh of her arms, and I wonder what else fled down those tracks with that strength.

"I don't even know why I love it so much," she says. "But you know how it is..." Her voice trails off hopefully. I nod and fix my gaze on the object of her desire. The lines of the piece are chunky and awkward, and the colors are gaudy and harsh. But in the way of my profession, my eyes smooth the fat lines into feathers and sweep the garish colors into fire. I wait for a moment while the wyrd, the holy purpose of it settles over me like a warm cloak. I see what she wants. She wants to be reborn while she still has the time.

"What's your name?" I ask her.

"Diane. Holling," she stammers. "Diane Holling."

I look up at her and conceal my pity for the sake of her pride. "I can do it, but you'll have to give me an hour or so to draw it up and get the studio ready." I gesture toward the lobby with my empty hand. "Go out there and tell Sophie you need to sign a release form."

She smiles at me, and it is sunlight. Her hands unclasp and flutter to grasp mine in a grip that is both fragile and joyful. "Thank you so much," she says. "I'll come back in an hour." I hear my daughter rummaging for the appropriate paperwork as the woman runs out of the room. That girl is psychic, I swear.

A few minutes later, the outside door slams shut, and Sophie pokes her head into the room. Her spiky hair is a vibrant shade of red this week, and her cat eyes spectacles are perched just above her dainty nose ring. She is wearing a new shade of claret lipstick and a clingy, black velvet dress. I have long since given up the fight to get her to dress in sensible clothes for work, but what a pretty girl she is.

"You're going to do it, aren't you?"

I grin. "Yeah. How many people do you think I've tattooed over the years who *didn't* tell me they had HIV?"

"You're a good woman, Mom."

"Help me set up?"

"You know it."

She bustles behind me with bleach water and paper towels while I sketch the woman's phoenix on tracing paper. It will rise above the small of her back; its wings will brush the valley beneath her kidneys. I think of it shielding the center of power at the base of her spine, and my hand hovers over the tracing paper for a moment.

"May it be a strength to her. May it watch over her. May it keep her safe."

"So may it be." Sophie leans over my shoulder as she speaks. The patchouli of her perfume is warm with the sweat of her endeavors, and the aroma softens the sharp odor of bleach water in the air. She smiles at me and tosses a wad of towels into the trash.

"How old do you think she is?" she asks me.

"I couldn't tell you. She looks about my age, but it might just be the illness."

"Oh, Mom, how awful. Did you see her arms?"

"Yeah, I did. Her teeth are a mess, too. She must have been hooked for a long time."

"Mom?" Sophie jumps onto the table and looks down at me. "Does it run in families? The predic... predispo..." Her voice trails off.

"Predisposition?" I offer. She nods. "My therapist tells me that some studies indicate children of substance abusers have a higher likelihood of becoming users themselves, but she doesn't know whether that likelihood is genetic, or situational, or both."

"So even though he died when I was little, it doesn't matter. Dad might have passed the gene onto me." She is worried.

"Yes, he might have. But you can always choose." I take her hands in mine. "And I am always your friend, honey."

"Hurry up. She'll be back in a minute." She squeezes my hands, grins, and steps down from the table. She's a tough girl, my daughter. Like her mother, she is.

My work is always holy, but I never know whether or not Spirit motivates it until I hear the buzz of the needle become the whisper of voices. Sometimes they are guardians, sometimes ancestors, and sometimes the sounds are croaks, howls, roars, or screeches. Occasionally I am told a bit of history, and these earlier strains in the song of the wyrd inform my work. It is as though the needle is a voice, and the ink is the story it tells.

There is a vast but subtle difference between vision and

hallucination, and I'm sure that most people who hear voices really are crazy. I thought I was at first, but then I realized I heard things only when I had a needle in my hand. Ink and blood and steel draw the spirits to me, and they don't come every time. I've tattooed thousands of people over the course of the last twenty-five years, and only a few hundred of those canvases had what I refer to in my mind as the ghost brush. I don't entirely know why they come, these ghosts, but I know that my work is never what I envision beforehand when they depart from it, and it is almost always an intimate manifestation of my clients' personhood. It makes them stronger.

Just after I wrap the lamp in plastic, and just before I put on my gloves, I call Sophie back in from the lobby. She does not speak to me, but she lifts an old knife from its display rack on the studio wall. I think it's from the war of 1812; I found it buried in my garden a while back and put it among the other artifacts in my studio. Something tells me it drowned in the blood it spilled and was forgotten, but I can't tell from looking at it whether that blood was Canadian or American. Perhaps it guards my Eastern wall now as payment for the sins of its former master. I occasionally think I hear him mourning.

Sophie faces the direction of the rising sun. I stand behind her and raise my hands while she calls the winds.

"Blow the guilt away from her mind!" Her voice is a contralto growl, and her arm sweeps the blade in a wide, five-pointed arc.

I turn to the South and lift the stained glass out of my favorite oil lamp. My sister made it for me long before her work was valued, or even good, for that matter. But I can think of no more fitting testament to the light of the soul than the work of her hands. I say, "Rekindle the flame in her spirit."

"Cleanse the sickness out of her blood." Sophie is already in the West. I put one hand on her shoulder and the other around the mug of salt water she clutches in her fingers. She smiles up at me, and the expression on her face is both joyful and sad. We put the mug back on the shelf together.

In the North, there is a glass fishbowl full of stones I've collected over the years. Most are just rocks, but there are a few chunks of quartz, hematite, and the like interspersed among the rest. I gather a handful and hold them close to me. "Root her in health," I say.

The front door creaks open, and the screen door slams shut.

"The circle is cast." Sophie winks at me and dashes into the lobby. I drop the stones back in the bowl and go to wash my hands. We don't consecrate the studio for every customer, but I think Diane needs all the help she can get. I'm glad Sophie agrees.

* * *

Black ink creates a void that begs to be filled with color. Diane's skin is puffy and hot in the places my needle has been, and an outline is emerging from the dark red smear I occasionally wipe away with soap and water. I spray her back with the solution, and she gasps.

"Do you keep that stuff in the freezer?" she asks me. "It feels so good."

"Yeah. And I can see your skin sizzle when I use it." I am joking, and she cracks an eye open and looks up at me.

"Well, keep it up." She grins and settles back into the cradle of her arms.

I've been listening since she lay down, and I am grateful that her lack of self-confidence prevents her from being chatty. Not that I mind conversation, but in these cases it's better to listen to the needle than it is to listen to the canvas. Although this time I'm seeing and feeling as much as I'm hearing. At first it is the eyes, wide like a Hentai heroine but set in the face of a child, anxious

7

and terrified and bruised. Then I see what she is looking at, a massive, blonde-haired shape made blurry by her tears. Finally, my groin begins to ache, an alien stretching that intensifies until I have to lift the needle and wait for it to pass. A knot of rage settles in my belly. I know what happened to her.

Then there is an older sound, a whisper of something not in the body, a wound or a sadness brought over from before. It sounds like the knife on my wall; it keens. I feel myself rocking with it like an old Irish woman and stop. That's just what she needs, an artist with a sharp needle and a penchant for chair dancing. I don't know where the keening comes from; I can't see it. But it's older than she is, and she brought it with her when her soul came back. I can't bring myself to believe that she deliberately reincarnated in a home with a sicko father figure to work out some obscure point of karma; the Universe just doesn't work that way. But she would have blamed herself for the rape, just like her soul blamed itself for whatever she brought into this life, and she may well have ridden the guilt train all the way to a needle fixation.

The outline is done. "Need a break?" I ask her.

"I could use one."

"Have you eaten?"

"I had breakfast."

The lobby door opens. I hear Sophie open the cash register and talk to someone young and male. A few seconds later, she pokes her head into the studio.

"Pizza, anyone?" she asks. Have I mentioned that my daughter is psychic?

"You should have some. You're burning endorphins."

Diane lifts up onto her elbows and adjusts her bra. "Should I put my shirt on?"

"Nah," Sophie tells her. "You're the last client today. Nobody here but us ink sluts." She grins and walks out.

Diane is more confident now, or perhaps we've just made her comfortable. I like to think we do that for most people. The tattoo industry is full up with self-important assholes who figure you should worship their needles. And most of them have posses far bigger than their talent. Me, I have pictures of Sophie from every year of her life cut and pasted together into a massive collage on one wall, a wolf's pelt a friend of mine bought at a flea market and brought to me because I'd "know how to honor its spirit" on another, a hundred or so pictures of my best tattoos glommed together like Sophie's collage, and my ancient Chihuahua Chile, who I've had since she was born in my bathtub, asleep under the sink. This is my home, and I want for my clients to feel good about being here, even if it does look a little like Marie Laveau's House of Voodoo meets Rembrandt.

"Oh, that was good." Diane is licking her fingers and looking for a napkin. I squirt some soap and water on a paper towel and hand it to her. "Yay! Freezer soap." she says, and sits down on the tattoo table to wipe her face and hands. "Ready for me?"

"Yep. Lie down and roll over," I tell her, and she does. "Now we color you in."

If black ink creates a void, then color calls into being. There is yellow first. I work from light to dark so her highlights aren't smeared by her shadows. The needle is a brush stroke now, and I know from my own experience under it that it scrapes the wounded places between her black lines. She is squinting, and her lips are a hard line, but her arms and legs are relaxed. That's the best way to take trauma, even if it is self-inflicted. The outer edges of her phoenix are orange with blood and ink now, but the color is going in remarkably well. Yellow is usually a bitch, but I don't think I'll have to re-touch this.

I begin to smell something earthy and sweating and surreptitiously sniff my pits. It's not me, and it's not her, and Sophie has taken the leash and gone out with Chile. In any case, the smell is

9

bigger than a Chihuahua and less refined than human sweat. There is a flash of gray in front of my eyes. I lift the needle and blink, and then I hear a throaty rumble somewhere between my inner ear and my brain. I want to get up and pace the room around her. I want to protect her with my teeth and claws. I mourn for her illness, but I refuse to abandon her. I am loyal. I am her mother. I put the needle to her skin again and close my teeth in front of my tongue to keep from panting. Step right up, ladies and gentlemen, and see the chair-dancing tattoo artist shape shift into a werewolf right before your very eyes. I am reminded of the pelt on my wall, and I am glad that her spirit is warded.

I am finished with the orange middle of her piece, and I have rinsed my needles and dipped them into the red. This is for the center of the small of her back, this core of fire, this color that cannot be distinguished from the blood she sheds for it. She is straining against her impulse to flee from pain; her hands are clenched into fists, and her breathing is gently labored. Her history is serving her well now, I think. How many times in our lives do we get to choose the pain we'll endure? I think of my clients. Most of them are accustomed to pain, but they all are grateful that the evidence of the suffering they endure here is beautiful.

I am warm, too warm, and I wipe my brow on my sleeve before continuing. I wonder how long her body will endure; HIV patients live long lives these days, not like when I was younger. Sophie returns with the dog and places a bottle of water on my workstation. I smile my thanks and continue brush-stroking the heart of this phoenix into being. My heart knows that Diane won't ever be an old woman, and I suddenly know what it is about her that Sophie finds compelling. There but for the grace of the Goddess... I am glad that I raised her carefully, that she saw and sympathized with the pain of others, that her life was full of line and color. She's a good girl; she's smart. She sees beneath the surface.

The warmth is heat now, but I am invigorated by it. Diane seems stronger too, and I know the heat is hers. Several seasons flash in front of my eyes, and I smell the ocean, and apples, and earth, and wood smoke. There is a kind of peace in these seasons, and good work in a place where her illness is useful to others. There are no more needles, and there is no more guilt. But the scars remain, the ones she chose and the ones she did not choose. After a time there is light, and freedom, and the chance to try again, but that's true of life no matter what comes after the body dies.

Her back burns, and I soothe it with soap and water. While she returns from that deep inner shelter where pain is endured, I wash my tools and silently thank them for their service to me.

"How does it look?" she asks.

"See for yourself." I help her up from the table and lead her to the mirror. She faces away from it and twists around. Her eyes widen and pool with tears.

"It's beautiful. It's so beautiful. I can't believe it."

Sophie comes in wearing latex gloves and carrying a roll of paper towels.

"Go into the washroom and let Sophie help you clean that up, then come back in and I'll bandage you." I grin, but I remember not to show pity. She isn't healed yet.

When I arrived, this is what she said.

"Lie down in my salt-spattered pine needles
and listen, your ear to the earth,
for the languages speaking in my bones;
Mi'kmaq, Gàidhlig, French, English,
these are the voices of your welcome.

"And come, oh daughter of too many journeys,
gray in your hair, lead in your heart,
sore-footed and stumbling, to the sea,
where we will weep together; stone, salt and water
until your sorrow erodes into sand.

"There is an ocean hidden in your veins,
a coyote in your mind, an oak in your belly,
a sparrow in the hollow of your throat.
Bring them here, to the ragged edge of the continent,
to your home, and set them free."

Hephaistos

He shuffles to the forge,
his leg a lead weight,
leaning hard on a gnarled stick,
and remembers the blows.

One from Hera,
who cast him from her womb into the sea -
and sits unbound now -
on a throne of his design.

He does not look to the mountain -
but with his God-ears hears -
the chiming chatter of his kin -
fall like shattering glass.

One from Aphrodite,
false gift, who left Ares' seed on the sheets -
and wears the net of her betrayal -
like a maiden's money-girdle.

His face is a melted mask, and -
his root-thick hands, sooty and shining -
reach into the firelight -
to begin the work of the day.

One from Athena,
with whom he shares the smith-craft,
whose only use for him -
was the hammer-blow that birthed her.

Then, from the hollow of the earth,
the sound of metal upon metal -
rings out of the darkness,
and the grace of Making comes.

Ammonite Baby

I DREAM OF HIM AGAIN, my ammonite boy, my Fibonacci spiral soul-son, the child my spirit already knows. This time he is two; his unkempt brown-black hair hangs loose over the collar of a thrift store shirt; his green eyes flash gleefully as he tosses his underwear out of the living room window and runs, shrieking with laughter, toward the back door. Damp with sweat and sleepy, I ease into wakefulness and slip my hand into my boxer shorts, musing about the particulars of his conception and the fecund roundness of his pregnant mother, a woman I do not yet know.

The woman next to me sighs in her sleep and turns onto her back. She is a pretty, firm thing and sails like a ship in a stiff breeze. She eats my cooking too, validates my politics, and shares a generic variety of my Hindu-Druidic-Pan-Polytheism. But I've been trying to give her something north of my belt buckle for at least two months now and just can't. I keep thinking we ought to split up before she gets too attached, but then she bends over my backyard garden in a pair of cut-off shorts or slides out from beneath the covers in her sleep, and I am suddenly convinced that today is not the day make waves.

By the time I am out of the shower, the coffee is ready, and a poached egg pan is filled with water and heating on the stove. Her massage tools are packed, and a thin line of herbs in little gelatin capsules waits for me on the counter. I scoop them up, pop them in en masse, and slug them down with a swig of warm coffee.

"I'll be late getting in tonight," she shouts from the bathroom down the hall. "Sarah Piggot just came home from the hospital, but her son is adjuncting for two different colleges this fall and doesn't have time to bring her in. I'm going to take the table over to their house this evening and treat her there. She shouldn't be out and about this soon anyway; she's too frail."

"Sounds good. Are you staying at your place then?"

"Yeah. Do you mind?"

"Not at all."

She turns the water on, and I return to the preparation of breakfast. There are mangoes in my fruit basket, and I peel and slice one, licking my juice-covered fingers as I go. By the time Kristen is finished, there are plates of food on the table, and she tucks in with the same gusto she brings to every physical thing. Her hair is a damp ponytail smelling of aloe and soap, and her round, clean face glows with the recent warmth of her shower.

"Should you be working today?"

"I don't think I'm contagious anymore; I'm not running a fever." She grins. "But I'll put a pot of Echinacea tea on in the waiting room and take a thermos to Sarah. It can't hurt anyway. How are you feeling?"

"I never catch anything."

We spend the remainder of our meal in silence. She looks comfortable to me, but the quiet certainly isn't companionable for both of us. We have to part company soon, but not this morning.

It would be cruel to break up with her before work on a Thursday. I resolve to do it tomorrow evening and make pleasant overtures of goodwill as she departs for the day. Inside an hour she is out the door, and my world belongs to me again, at least for a while.

I pass the day and evening in front of my computer banging out crappy word after crappy word until I give up, order a pizza, and throw myself down in front of the late show. There's a deadline looming over my head, but there's no muse while the Kristen thing looms there with it. Half a pie and three beers later the bedroom is too far to travel, and I fall asleep on the sofa.

This time my ammonite baby is a girl, and she is a gangly twelve. Almost a young lady but not quite, she divides her time between amateur astronomy and the science of makeup. Her mother's hands are slender, capable cosmetic wands that brush color over the lids of long-lashed, emerald eyes impatient to open and look at me, impatient to gaze with me through the lens of our telescope and up at the stars. The cells of my body ache with thankfulness that she allowed me to bring the house of her bright soul into being, to cradle it in my arms, to teach it to walk, to read, wonder at the universe.

When I open my eyes, the living room is dim with the first grey light of a cloudy morning. I inhale the fragrance of imminent rain as the wind blows it in through my open windows and allow myself to sob quietly into the sofa cushion. Who is this soul that so needs me, and why does it play my body like an old, firm hand on an ancient drum? How is it that I can miss this child I have never met, look forward to its infrequent visits to my dreamtime, and long for sleep when it comes back to me after a long absence? I return to fitful slumber until the phone wakes me.

"Daniel?"

"Yeah, Kristen. What's up?"

"I'm taking the day off from work. Can I bring you some lunch in a few hours?"

"Sure. Is everything all right?"

She is quiet for a moment. "Yeah, Daniel. Everything is fine. Can we talk about it over lunch?"

"Absolutely. See you then."

I put the phone back on the receiver and sit up. Well, we were going to break up today anyway. Satisfied, I grab the half-empty pizza box, go to my computer, and type contentedly until noon.

* * *

"I'm pregnant." She holds up a shaking hand to stop me from speaking, which is good, because I can't breathe anyway. "Look, I already know we don't care for each other in the same way, so don't feel like you have to commit more than you can..."

"I thought it was the flu." Now that was an idiot thing to say.

She raises an eyebrow and frowns. "It was the flu. I took the pregnancy test last night after I stopped running a fever but kept feeling queasy. Do you think I would lie to you about something like this or...or withhold it from you until it was too late and then force you into fatherhood? Damn it, Daniel. I already told you that you were transparent as plastic wrap. Do you really think I'd super-glue myself to somebody who only wants me for my pussy?"

"It's not like that."

"It is precisely like that." She stands up and paces the room, her hands clenched at her sides. "For shit's sake Daniel, you wallow in your very own personal swamp. You brood and whine and let your house fall apart and your garden go to seed and...and why on earth would I want to..." She stops, clamps a hand over her mouth, and shudders.

I jump to my feet and pull her into my arms. After a few moments, she sinks into me and begins to weep quietly. "Stop placating me," she whispers into my shoulder.

"I'm not placating you." My head bends toward her and my lips rest on the crown of her head for a moment. "I should have told you how I felt. Of course you'd figure it out all by yourself; you're not stupid."

"No, I'm not."

"What do you want to do now?"

She looks up at me; her eyes are red and swollen, and a few dark strands of hair are plastered to her cheek.

"It's your child too. What do you want? Do you want anything at all?"

I take her hands in mine and pull her over to the sofa. "Oh no. Kristen, this is your body. You should be the one to choose."

"But I don't want to burden you..."

It's my turn to get up and pace. My foot lands on an elastic my cat dragged into the living room some days ago, and I pick it up and wrap it around my hair, cinching it into a tight ponytail. The rain has long ago passed over, so I re-open the windows and pull the curtains back. A clean, damp scent drifts in on the breeze, and I drop to my knees and breathe it in. The clouds are still heavy overhead, but streaks of sunlight are staining the grass gold, and the willow tree in my backyard is bent over the garden, its dripping leaves gracing my cabbages with droplets of extra moisture.

"Why don't we cast a circle and do a reading for it?" I ask her and turn around to watch her response. Her brows wrinkle as she thinks about it, but her body is relaxed. "I'm not sure what to think right now, and I could use the grounding. I imagine you could too. You could throw the coins, and I could throw the runes, and we could see what we see. It's going to be a pretty night."

"We could put some acorn squash in the oven beforehand, and then we'd have a hot meal when we're done," she says and nods her head. "I think it's a good idea."

So we pass the late afternoon chatting about everything but those things that matter most. Sarah Piggot is recovering nicely, but her son is neck deep in student papers. My novel is coming along as well as can be expected, but it's not my best work. The garden is flourishing now that the weeds are gone...and then the conversation draws too near the precipice, so we both back away.

It begins to rain again at dusk, and we are forced to retrieve our blanket and candles from underneath the willow tree. I worry the weather shift has disrupted the precarious balance of energy between us; we say little while we toss the blanket in the dryer, put dinner in the oven, and move the living room furniture out of the way. She has retreated into some unapproachable place; I sense the buzz of pain on her surface, but she is not present in it. I haven't known her long enough to cope with this mood, so I do not address it and hope instead that she comes back before we begin.

And she does, a bit. By the time the living room walls are bathed in candlelight and the air is hazy with sage, she is solid and warm and present. But there is uncertainty in her magic; she goes to the East, her coins in her hands, and opens her mouth to speak but can't. I follow her lead and bow to the Air, not wanting to chase her back into herself by calling the wrong energy or saying the wrong thing. She sighs and moves to the South, closing her eyes as she is settles into that place. I bow again and wait. In the West I bend to address the Water, and my blood stirs for a moment in the hollow, flat place above my groin. I try to pull the energy up along the soul-roads of my body, but it lodges in my chest and will not travel any farther. In the North she clasps her hands around her belly, but I cannot touch her, will not touch her, and my bow to the Earth is perfunctory at best.

She sits down in the center of the circle and pulls her books off of the coffee table and onto the floor. After a moment or two of meditation, she casts the coins, marking out the broken and unbroken lines of the oracle in her journal as she goes. I follow her example in this too, closing my eyes and gathering the components of my question until they are a single mass in my mind. When I am ready, I untie the little bag of runes from my belt and reach inside it, stroking my intent into their smooth surfaces. Before she is finished I am pulling them out; one, two, and three to begin. Hagalaz, Laguz reversed, and Inguz. Well...I don't need to be told that I'm afraid and closed off, but there is wisdom enough in Inguz, so it becomes the cornerstone of a second casting; Inguz, Raido, Mannaz, and Laguz again, upright. Kristen sighs and closes her journal, looking up at me.

"Chien changes to Wu Wang," she says, exasperated. "In short, nothing."

"Me neither. But I'm pretty sure the runes think I have an emotional block."

"I could have told you that."

"What are you getting from the coins?"

"Well, Chien talks about emotional barriers too and the futility of getting stuck behind them. It advises no forward movement but does suggest that I might find some clarity in counseling. In any case, it doesn't speak to this situation, since we have to make a decision soon. Wu Wang is about innocence, not forcing an issue, and letting things resolve themselves, which also doesn't help us, and for the same reason. What've you got?"

"Me, me, and more me. Hagalaz and Laguz reversed are about the emotional block thing, and there's an element of fear and disruption probably associated with your pregnancy. Inguz is a little different; common convention associates it with sacrifice and work for the betterment of home and family, but I've always seen it as the quintessential husband rune. I thought maybe they were telling me to do whatever you thought was best, to be supportive. My second reading seemed to indicate that doing the right thing and acting in a supporting role would relieve me of the emotional burden, which made sense to me but still didn't answer my question."

"Sounds like a cop-out to me," she says and looks down at her hands, fumbling with the silver rings she always wears. "I still don't know what to do."

"And I can't tell you, Kristen. "But I will support whatever decision you make."

"That's the problem," she says, and her eyes well with tears. "You'll support the decision, but you can't support the decision-maker." She runs her fingers through her hair and looks away. "I don't know if I can bear a child under these circumstances; I don't think I can be a good mom and say good things about a dad who never...who never loved me."

For the second time in a day, her words have reduced me to silence. There is a strange, throbbing knot in my chest where my Kundalini is hammering against the place where Laguz sits reversed over my heart. So I say nothing at all and wait for her to start packing her things away. And then we take the circle down, each of us locked in our own private uncertainty, farther apart now than we were when we began. But dinner is good, and when the hour grows late, I offer her the bed and make camp on the couch again. Perhaps we'll know more in the morning.

This time there is a green-eyed grandchild, and all I see is her gap-toothed grin and baby hands that reach out to grab onto my gray ponytail and beard. I hear a voice in the kitchen; I can't tell if it's male or female, but it carries the same resonant quality mine does. There is a crisp, clean quality to the sunlight that filters into the room and a new chill in the air. It might be Mabon, or it might be my birthday; they fall so close together. In any case, this grand-baby's grandmother comes to fetch her away from me and drop her securely onto a matronly hip that still makes my prick ache, even after all this time. My ammonite baby has an ammonite baby, and the spiral that brought mine to me continues down and down into the bare-footed poppet whose fingers are never too tight around her grandpa's hair, and down and down into her poppets and theirs, long after I have gone to be with my Mother for good. In that moment it is all right to die; there is a curve on my granddaughter's chin that comes from me and will always be like mine, just like her emerald eyes will always resemble her grandmother's.

There is no consolation for me in the morning. Kristen is in the kitchen, and there is an old milk crate on the table full of vitamins, cosmetics, and clothes. I force the dream to recede and address the evidence of her departure.

"I have decided to terminate the pregnancy," she tells me, and folds a sweater on top of the crate. "But I think this should be the last time we see each other. I'll let you know how everything goes after I've taken care of it."

"Oh, please let me pay for this; please let me come with you." The words are out before they can be censored. "Please let me be a friend to you, even if I can't be anything else. Please."

She looks at me and frowns. "I don't need your pity and don't want your money."

"All right, you don't. But you should let me pay for half of this, and you should let me help out around the house. Honestly Kristen, I know I haven't been fair to you, but don't shut me out altogether. You may need me."

She looks at me for a long moment. "Bring me dinner sometime this week," she says as she puts her sunglasses on. "I have to get home and mow the lawn. See you later."

And then she is out the door, crate in hand, and gone from me.

I make dinner for her twice a week during the next month

while we wait for her scheduled appointment. She is frequently nauseous when I see her; early pregnancy isn't kind to her stomach. There are lots of saltines and fresh tomato soup from the garden, a few chicken pot pies, and more than one evening of vanilla ice cream and 'thank you' but nothing else. In the meantime, I start running a fever, clogging up at the nose and throat, and vomiting on a somewhat regular basis. We play a lot of poker on those nights when she allows me to visit, and as the end of our time together draws near, I find myself stopping at the bank to cash in five and ten dollar bills for quarters and dimes, since my spare carboy has long since been emptied by my apparent inability to manufacture a game face. At some point during our sojourn together, I realize that I will miss her when she's gone, but I don't tell her this. She's under enough stress without having to deal with my fickle emotional proclivities.

And so the day comes like any other, and by the time we come to it, we are at least friends. She has slept and showered at my house for the first time in weeks, and we chat amiably over breakfast; I am finally kicking my novel's ass, and she is looking forward to the two-week vacation she is about to take. We make our way to the truck, and she volunteers to drive so that she can run down any protesters we encounter in the parking lot, but I decorously refer to her delicate condition and refuse to allow her behind the wheel. There is a sense of the holy in the rustle of my willow branches and the late summer bees that wander out of my vigorous hives and into the goldenrod at the edge of the field; I think briefly of autumn honey mead and turn my attention to the garden. I really ought to start gathering in the harvest. I'm not eating my tomatoes and squashes fast enough now that Kristen spends most of her time in town, and I don't want the food to go to waste.

As it turns out, it's an off-day for the protesters; the clinic is a place of quiet competence when we arrive. I am immediately ignored by the queue of receptionists, accountants, and nurses that seem to line up in front of her, each one asking a different question, each one requiring a different response. She manages them with characteristic candor, but as with the circle we cast together, there is hesitation in her magic; I can sense it. There is something behind her eyes, behind her voice, in the clumsy way she knocks her keys and wallet to the floor while signing her name to the registration form. I know better than to press her now, but I hope...I pray there is strength in the center of the place I fear is hollow, that place where I should be as she makes this journey. I still don't know how to approach this mood, so when we are finally settled in for the wait, I withdraw as well and turn my face toward the window and the distant hum of passing traffic. Before long she is squeezing my hand and rising out of the chair. There is a woman waiting at the door, but I cannot bring myself to look at her, and then Kristen is gone from me again.

A blur of people pass by on foot; they seem so far away from me, from the clinic, from this experience. Kristen shouldn't be alone right now; she should never have been alone, but she is far away now too, and she probably won't ever return. There is still the woman in my dreams though, her round belly, her slender hands, and the child who already loves me. They are with me, always with me, even now. My jaw clenches, and my eyes brim with tears. Who is here with Kristen? Who knows her heart today? What dream guides her behind that gateway, down that hall, in that white, empty room?

Three minutes pass, and there comes a copper-bright shape to the door where she has gone. Faceless, almost formless, and too soon to be my Kristen returned from her passage, it shines with a towering, writhing, queenly darkness that burns the side of my face still turned toward the street and forces me to look and to see what has risen up out of the place I feared was empty. I get up from the chair and in that moment realize she is Kali, the one

25

who creates and the one who destroys. It is clear that on this day she has chosen to create, and I who am Shiva bow my head and clasp her hands to my breast in honor of her choice. No longer is this my Mystery; it is hers. Mine came before and will come after, but today I am her acolyte. I look down into the pools of her tears and my blood screams a recognition so profound that it dissolves the knot in my chest in an instant, and I am faint with the energy that rushes up through my heart, my throat, my head. I pull her hands around my waist, and she leans against me, clasping her hands behind my back. I never before realized her eyes were so green.

Stefanos

Broken like a shaman on the rock of his journey –
Prometheus in love with his pain –
I know where you are.

We come of age and know we cannot abandon you -
without abandoning ourselves.
There are only so many saviors.

I sat on that rock a long time ago and bled awhile.
The birds picked at my liver too.
I remember their little beaks.

But I got up one day and went away from that place.
I stole fire; I can cut a fucking chain.
The birds went hungry that day.

Get up off of that altar; your sacrifice is not required.
Use your slender, clever fingers -
to steal your life back.

The Interstitial Fairy Demolition Crew Casts a Circle

Where the highway bends its shoulder -
into heaping piles of trash,
where the warehouse hulks, abandoned -
baring teeth of broken glass,
where the concrete cracks and crumbles -
like a scab upon the soil,
and Blue Flax mingles in the wrack -
with Scarlet Sage and Cinquefoil,

There the dark sidhe, born in cities -
murmur their destructive prayers -
for bottle shards and brittle plastic,
rusting bumpers, flattened tires.
There they sow a creeping ivy -
over buildings thus defiled,
and call the wolves to come and wander -
in those places, newly wild.

In the East (Somewhere Near St. Clair Shores):

28

Now comes Smoke Stack to begin,
gray and gritty son of Wind,
and ask his mother for a boon.
"Bring the cleansing tempest soon:

"Guardian of the East, Watchtower of Air,
gather my corruption into your lungs,
flay it from my body and blow me out,
a white death wind, a fury that rends.
So mote it be."

And the host echoes, "So mote it be."

In the South (Inside the Detroit-Windsor Tunnel):
Now comes Gas Line to the game,
canny keeper of the Flame -
to beg her mother's charity.
"Make the city burn with me:

"Guardian of the South, Watchtower of Fire,
caress, with your flickering fingers,
the fissures where I whisper out,
aching to be set alight, to rage bright.
So mote it be."

And the host echoes, "So mote it be."

In the West (Between Novi and Walled Lake):
Now comes Acid Rain to weep,
bitter daughter of the Deep,
and call her mother's killing flood.
"Bathe the pavement in your blood:

"Guardian of the West, Watchtower of Water,
spit me like a poison onto the boulevard,
and drench the rot my spatter quickens;
a slick, brown spray, a sweet decay.
So mote it be."

And the host echoes, "So mote it be."

In the North (Atop the Empty Chrysler Factory in
    Pontiac):
Now comes Weed to climb the wall,
green-limbed cleric of the Fall,
and lift his leaves up to the sun.
"Mother Earth, thy will be done:

"Guardian of the North, Watchtower of Earth,
shepherd the whiskered scavengers here,
sweep the winged beasts to my shelter;
a cave and aerie, a sanctuary.
So mote it be. The circle is cast."

And the host echoes, "So mote it be. The circle is cast."

Their voices die, and in the gap -
between that moment and the next,
Air and Water, Fire and Earth -
descend from their exalted rest -
to bless the host and move upon -
the city, heavy with disease;
a zephyr breath, a morning dew,
a shaft of light, a flight of bees -

that bring the succor of the world -

to all the kindred ravaged there;
the withered oak, the riven deer,
the blighted fae absorbed in prayers,
which echoed, as a threnody,
their mothers' elemental woe -
for children past the reach of hope,
whose sorrow we will never know.

From Our Minds to Yours

I AM BURNING SAGE, as much as I can stand to breathe. The glassworks is redolent with it, and I can see the Bling beginning to tear up. One woman is clutching a handkerchief she pulled from the black, leather handbag that broke Maya's phoenix. The other is edging toward the door. Sage is hard to come by anymore unless you grow it yourself; you can't buy it in bulk like you could in my mother's day. So I'm squandering a little of my garden to get rid of them. They don't look like buyers to me though, and I don't want them to break anything else.

"Do you make these?" the handkerchief bearer approaches the counter and gestures at the gallery, where clouds of sunlit smoke wreathe a menagerie in glass. Her lips stretch into a Carmine Rose smile, and she tucks a loose strand of Ash Brown #5 behind her ear.

"No, the shop belongs to a friend of mine." I cross my arms under my breasts and inhale, settling into my best 'impassive black woman' posture. It's a technique that often works for me in court, given my taller than average stature and somewhat masculine features. I'm hoping it will discourage her from making conversation.

The woman hesitates for a second and then says, "Oh. So you just work here."

"Only when she needs a hand."

"Oh. And she lets you burn...whatever it is you're burning?"

I grin. "Sage has a cleansing vibration."

"Oh." The handkerchief bearer departs. Her compatriot is actively seeking exodus now. A moment later they're gone, so I open the doors and windows.

They hate to be called Bling. They say it's offensive and old-fashioned, but I think it's accurate. They come out of their corpo-villages smelling of car leather and canned atmosphere, swipe their credit cards a few times and cart their slum treasure home in shiny, electric sedans. To be fair, most are decent people, and I've provided legal representation to more than a few. But they're Inside, where medical care is consistent and superior, where markets still carry almost everything they used to and where the village Intranet shapes their vision of the world. We're Outside, where many no longer have access to medicine, where we grow or barter for much of our food and where we have whatever Internet we can afford. I'm lucky; I have a good education and a wealthy family, so I can live and work wherever I want. Most don't have that choice.

The back door opens. "You've had Bling today!" Maya shouts forward.

"How can you tell?" I shout back.

"You smoked them out."

"They broke your phoenix!"

"No! That piece took me hours. Did they pay for it?"

"Of course not."

"Girls, put your sweaters away and go say hello to your Aunt Adande."

There is a rustling of fabric and then a thunder of girl feet into the gallery. Fran is twelve and young for her age, a black-haired beauty of a child, and her younger sister Sammi is quiet, tough, ten going on thirty. I meet them halfway to slow them down, and they fling their arms around me.

"How did it go?" I look up at their mother.

She tosses me the car keys and shakes her head. Salt and pepper wisps fall over her brow. "He was good with them. He listened while they told him about their nightmares. He asked what prompted their interest in Peridyne toys and suggested they play with cheaper alternatives. Then he recommended we spend more time together and told us to use our imaginations."

"So he was useless, and he didn't tell you anything you didn't already know."

"He was kind, and he didn't know what to do."

"How much did he charge you for his kindness?"

"Adande, please."

I sigh and release the girls, who go into the back room to play. "I'm sorry. I know this is hard."

"And please don't smoke my customers out anymore."

"They broke your..."

"I know; you told me. But were they interested in anything else?"

I think about the question. "Not that I can remember," I tell her, "and I'm sorry for that, too. I'll try to be more...approachable when I watch the shop."

Maya laughs aloud, lays a slim, white hand on her midriff and sits down. When she looks up at me, her gray eyes are merry. "Yes, that's you my love, approachable."

"You should see me in court."

The girls begin to sing a Peridyne jingle, and Maya sobers.

"Why don't you let me take them back into the village and buy them a few things?" I ask her.

"Because I don't love you for your income, that's why, and because our lives aren't about the things we own."

"But if it will calm them…"

She reaches out and draws me toward her. "Teach them to play chess."

"Okay." I wrap my arms around her shoulders, lean down and lay my chin on her head. "But I still feel partly responsible for this. If I hadn't taken them into the village, they wouldn't have known what they were missing."

The girls are loud now, and the jingle is feverish. They burst into the room. Fran tugs at her mother's sweater.

"Will you take us into Peridyne _now_, Mom?"

"First of all, when did 'please' drop out of your vocabulary? And second, there isn't anything to play with in Peridyne that we can't duplicate here. We've already talked about this."

"Yes, we know." Sammi pushes her sister aside and steps forward. "You can't afford Peridyne toys, and the behavioral specialist told us to learn to play with what we have. But we _need_ them, Mother."

"Why do you need them, Sammi?" I ask her, kneeling down.

"Because it hurts us not to have them."

I glance up at Maya, who nods her head in the affirmative. "It's what they say every time I ask them."

"How does it hurt you?" I wrap my dark, weathered fingers around their perfect, pale hands and look into their eyes, so like their mother's.

"It just does," Fran answers, and begins to sing again.

* * *

My car is crowded with people and food, and my trunk is full of witchery. There is a cascade of conversation falling over me; the community garden vis-à-vis the fucked-up weather, the fossil fuel statute. There is magical talk as well; the work of this evening's Moon, Beltane planning, the new rune set Sylph is making for Fran. It's a soothing thing, this friendly babble, and it loosens the knot of worry around my heart.

"How did the doctor's visit go today?" Sylph reaches up and puts her hand on my shoulder.

I glance into the rearview mirror at her freckled face and blue eyes. "He told them to spend more time together and to use their imaginations."

"What a crock." Her nose wrinkles. "How are the girls?"

"They're still having nightmares and singing Peridyne jingles."

"And you think this is happening because you took them to the mall?"

"I don't know. I can't imagine where else they could have seen Peridyne-branded toys. Not even I can find them outside the village or the Intranets, and I've got subscriptions to Peridyne and Microfield at work. The jingles I can understand. There's always some kind of music playing on the login screens, but you have to have a paid account to get into the online stores."

"Weird."

"Speaking of weird, you heard about Levi, right?" Dodge leans forward over his belly, and the beads on his silver beard braids click together.

"No. What happened to him?" Anni leans around to look at Dodge and rests an ancient hand on his knee. Her long, white hair loosens at her nape and falls over the collar of her blouse.

"He was caught in Peridyne two days ago stealing a blender."

My head jerks up. "A blender? What would a fifteen year-old boy want with a blender? And why didn't Matt call me?"

"I have no idea, and because he can't afford you. Besides, you don't do criminal law." Dodge strokes his braids and grimaces.

"He knows I'll barter with him, and I can defend Levi in a misdemeanor case."

"Tell him that yourself. He'll be there tonight, and so will the boy."

We arrive at Maya's house as the sun is setting. Matt's ethanol conversion is parked out front, and he is sitting on the porch. Dodge plugs my car in, greets Matt with a grip of the forearm and follows the others inside. I hang behind and sit down on the porch swing.

"I heard," I tell him.

"I thought Dodge would say something."

"Matt, I'll take repair work for payment, you know that."

"I wasn't going to ask."

"You should always ask."

"He's so torn up about this." Matt runs his hands over his close-cropped hair, and the fine lines around his dark eyes deepen as he frowns.

"How did he even get into Peridyne? It's a gated community."

"Well, my garage abuts the woods on one side, and the Peridyne mall abuts them on the other. He and the boys just cut through."

Levi opens the screen door, looks down at me and offers his hand. I shake it.

"I know you're probably talking to Dad about the blender I stole, and I didn't think he should have to talk to you by himself." He comes outside and sits on the porch railing. "Will you represent me, Ms. King? I can work it off in trade."

"That's very mature of you," I tell him. "I'll take your offer of trade under advisement, but I have already decided to represent you."

"Thank you," he says, and his shoulders sag.

"Why did you steal the blender, Levi?" I look up at him and rest my hands on the seat.

"I don't know." His voice quavers, and his eyes fill with tears. "I honestly don't. Me and Peter and Yarrow never went into Peridyne when we were kids; we just played in the woods behind the shop. And then about two months ago, we decided to check the place out. After that, I started having these awful dreams."

My fingers grip the swing reflexively, but I manage to keep the anxiety out of my voice. "You've had nightmares?"

"Yeah, they're really bad sometimes too. I'll be happy in them and be buying all kinds of things, and then I'll wake up and be... hungry for the stuff I dreamed about."

"You never told me about this." Matt stands up, and his rough hands reach out to his son. Levi allows himself do be embraced, and his long, blond hair falls over his father's shoulder. He sighs, rests there a moment and then steps back.

"Because it was stupid, Dad. What was I supposed to do, tell you I was craving Peridyne blenders?

Maya peeks around the screen door and smiles. "You guys about ready?"

I stand up and position myself between the men and my beloved, giving them a chance to regain their composure. "We'll be right in."

* * *

Levi's case is easier to resolve than I expect it to be; I am able to negotiate a three-week community service sentence after a single phone call to the Peridyne prosecutor. During the conversation though, I sense she's almost inclined to dismiss the case, not unusual for a first offense misdemeanor, but even so her tone strikes me as odd. I resolve to discuss the interaction with Matt, but when I call him I barely have the chance to announce myself and say a few words.

"Levi's dreams are getting worse," he interrupts me, "and he hasn't slept more than a few hours at a time since you saw him on Friday. He won't sleep alone in his room anymore either; he says he's afraid he'll go sleepwalking."

"Matt, that's horrible. Have you taken him to a doctor?"

"And have the doctor tell me the same thing he told Maya? I can't afford that. There's something else," he adds, lowering his voice, "I went into Peridyne yesterday to see the store where Levi stole the blender and ended up spending a week's earnings at the mall. I have no idea why I did it, and you'll never believe the crap I bought. But I haven't felt this good since I was popping Disco Biscuits, and I can't bring myself to take anything back. I've got it all stuffed into a box in the shop."

"What the hell is going on?" I lean back in my chair, take off my reading glasses and rub my eyes.

"I don't know, but I'm not sending my son back in there. I don't care what you've negotiated."

"Let me get back to you in a little while, all right? I want to check in on Maya and the girls and see how they're doing."

I dial her number at the shop, but nobody answers, so I dial her cell. By the time I get her voicemail, I am already in the car. I arrive at the glassworks to find it closed and speed on to her house a few blocks away. The police are out front, and Maya is standing on the porch wearing an old sweater and jeans. I don't see Fran and Sammi, but as I get out of the car I can hear them singing somewhere inside the house.

"What's going on?" I ask her as I run to the porch, but a stocky blonde officer in a Peridyne uniform intervenes.

"Who are you?" she asks.

"I'm her attorney," I reply, and look down at the woman.

"Now I'll ask again, and I expect an answer this time. What's going on?"

"The girls ran away this morning," Maya tells me, wiping her eyes on her sleeve. She has been crying a long time. "The Peridyne police found them outside the mall."

"I'm glad they're safe," I tell her and turn toward the officer. "Thank you for your help. Now, why are you still here, and why haven't you permitted my client the use of her cell phone?"

"My cell phone is inside. I heard it ring..."

"The children are being questioned by Child Protective Services. The parent is not permitted to be present."

"Are there police officers inside the house?"

"Yes," Maya answers. "Her partner took the girls in."

"Did you give her partner your specific consent to be there?" I ask her.

"I...I don't remember."

I move past her and open the screen door. Fran and Sammi are sitting in the living room with two middle-aged women in expensive business suits and pumps. There is a police officer in the kitchen, opening cabinets.

"You!" I point at the officer. "Do you have a warrant?"

He looks into the living room and walks toward me, a sausage-fingered hand on his holster. "Who are you?" he asks, raising a thick, black eyebrow.

"I am Maya Cleary's attorney, and I asked you if you have a warrant for the search you are currently conducting."

"She invited me in."

"Then why is she outside? No, I think it more likely that these women used their authority as agents of Child Protective Services to bully Maya, and you seized an opportunity to follow them into the house and conduct an unauthorized search."

"We have a legal right to question children we believe are in danger." One of the women walks toward me. I glare at her, and she stops.

"Their mother has a legal right to have her attorney present during that questioning." I answer. "So after this officer has shown me his search warrant, I will sit down with you."

"I apologize for the misunderstanding, ma'am. If you'll excuse me." The policeman slides past me and walks out of the house.

"Now," I turn my attention to the women, "you'll begin by telling me exactly what you've asked these children. After that, they'll be given the opportunity to tell me what has happened in their own words. When they've finished, you may proceed with your questions."

"I think we've satisfied ourselves that Fran and Sammi aren't in any _immediate_ danger." The second woman lifts her head and frowns.

"Excellent. Then you'll be going now." I follow them out and stand on the porch with Maya while her guests depart in their respective vehicles. When they have gone, she lays her head on my shoulder, and I wrap her in my arms.

"Thank you," she says simply, and then draws in a deep breath. "Let's go talk to the girls."

"I need to call Matt first," I tell her. "And you should speak with him before you go inside."

Levi is in the basement reading to Fran and Sammi out of a book of fairy tales he brought from home. I can hear his voice rising above the drone of the dishwasher, strong and sure despite his weariness. Maya is pouring tea out of a Japanese pot and slicing hot bread. Even under stress, she soothes and comforts the people around her, a magic I'm certain I'll never master. Matt takes a plate and cup from her, smiling his gratitude.

"I've been thinking about this," he says to Maya, "and I've made a list of things your family and mine have in common." He takes a bite of bread, opens a folded sheet of paper and invites us to follow his notes.

"Okay. We both have businesses near Peridyne, which means we both get village customers pretty regularly. The children were fine until they went into Peridyne, then they started to crave village products and have bad dreams. I went into Peridyne and felt like I had taken Ecstasy while I was shopping there." He looks at Maya. "Have you ever been to the village?"

"I went in once a couple of years ago to get nutmeg for a recipe, but I found it at the food co-op after that. I'm not comfortable in Peridyne," she adds. "But what about Adande? She goes in and out of there all the time."

"She also has the money to buy whatever she wants when she wants it, just like the people who live there." He turns to me. "Have you ever craved anything from Peridyne?"

"Well, as much as I like to complain about the place, you're right. I have the money to buy whatever I want, and I do shop there from time to time. But I wouldn't say there's anything in Peridyne I can't do without. What are you getting at?"

Matt sips his tea and puts his mug down. "This is going to sound crazy, but hear me out. I think Peridyne residents are being infected with something that makes them brand-loyal, something they shed. I think Maya and I have been exposed to it because we have shops near the village, and that's where the kids picked it up. I also think you've been exposed, but probably not to the same extent, and whatever cravings you might get are satisfied when you shop there."

"You mean like a virus?" I ask him. "What kind of virus would make you crave things only after you've seen them up close, drug you if you satisfy the craving and give you nightmares if you don't?"

"I don't know," he answers. "I'm not a doctor; I just know machines."

"Nanobots could do it. I've read about how they treat diseases and stuff." Levi is standing at the basement door, listening to us. "Can we have some bread? We can smell it all the way downstairs."

Maya tells Levi to get plates out of the kitchen cabinet, and I pause to consider what Matt has said. Suddenly, I begin to see connections between events; the prosecutor's eagerness to resolve Levi's case, the behavior of the Peridyne police and the visit from Child Protective Services.

"They don't know what's happening either." I murmur thoughtfully. "They've had more visitors from the Outside and an increase in crime, but they don't know why."

"How do we find out if Matt is right?" Maya asks.

"My sister is a nurse practitioner at the Microfield College clinic. Let me see if she has any ideas." I pull my cell phone from my handbag and dial Halla's number. When she answers, I give her the situation in brief.

"Adande, I know you don't approve of our lifestyle, but I can't believe you think Peridyne is deliberately addicting people to its products. That's just paranoid."

"I'm not prepared to argue with you about this. These children need medical attention their parents can't afford. If I bring them into the clinic and pay for their visits myself, will you examine them and do blood tests?"

"Of course I will. I have emergency walk-in hours tomorrow morning; you can bring them in then." She pauses. "And I'm sorry I said you were paranoid. If my friends' children were behaving as you've described, I'm not sure what I'd think."

"Thank you for saying so," I tell her, and end the call.

Microfield is a four-hour drive from Peridyne, so Matt and Levi stay at Maya's house overnight, and I collect the children early in the morning for the trip north. The girls are subdued; they're old enough to realize their behavior is hurting Maya but too young to fight their cravings and deal with their nightmares alone. So Levi reads to them all morning with the same weary courage he showed the night before, and I am moved once again by the quality of his character.

When we arrive, Halla's assistant ushers the children into separate examination rooms and asks me to wait outside. Halla is my younger sister by almost a decade, a polished, gracious woman like most of her neighbors, and with many of the same attitudes. She is compassionate with me and with the children though, examining each of them separately and listening to their concerns.

"Physically, they're fine," she tells me after she finishes. "But they're under quite a bit of stress. Whatever it is they're dealing with, it's upsetting them. Tell you what," she offers, "I have a colleague and friend in the Physical Sciences department who might have a microscope capable of seeing nanoparticles. If you like, I'll ask him to look at their blood samples. At least then we can rule out your concerns and move forward with diagnosis and treatment."

"Thank you, Halla. I really appreciate this."

"It's good of you to be so kind to them," she tells me, and there is an undertone in her compliment I choose to ignore.

The children and I do not stop for lunch in Microfield as we might otherwise have done. Instead, we wait until we are well outside of town and picnic in a public park while Levi finishes reading from his book.

"You're growing into a good man," I tell him afterward while the girls are taking turns on a nearby swing set.

"Thank you, Ms. King." He offers me a half-smile and looks over at Fran and Sammi. "But my dad was right about what's happening to us, and I think I'm right about what's causing it."

44

"What makes you think so?" I ask him.

"Nothing else makes sense, and I just feel it." He shrugs. "You won't be able to fix this, and neither will Dad or Maya."

"Don't give up on us yet," I tell him, and squeeze his arm.

He pulls away and stands up. "Some problems can't be solved, Ms. King," he tells me and then goes to play with the girls.

* * *

I am awakened at four o'clock the following morning by a hammering at my apartment door and open it to find Halla there. She is still wearing the same skirt and blouse she had on the morning before, and she looks tired and disheveled.

"Yusef looked at their blood," she tells me as I usher her into the kitchen and heat water for coffee. "Then he looked at his own. Then he called me, and we looked at mine. Then we looked at all the samples again under a different microscope. We wanted to be sure." She sits down at the table and puts her head in her hands. "He says we all have a significant number of nanoparticles in our blood."

"So Microfield is doing it as well." The kettle whistles, and I grind the beans for coffee. "I would imagine it's a widespread practice then. There are at least, what? Four corpo-communities per state on average? Two per province in Canada?"

"And several abroad. If that's Peridyne coffee, I don't want it," she tells me as I put a mug in front of her.

"Free Trade. I get it through the food co-op."

She wraps her fingers around the mug and takes a sip. "You should probably throw this mug out, scrub everything I've touched and toss your cleaning rags after I leave."

"What do you know about these nanoparticles?"

"Yusef told me they can only communicate over short distances, no more than a few meters."

45

"Which would explain why Matt and the children didn't have any symptoms until they first went into the mall."

"Perhaps. Your friend's euphoria might also be symptomatic; nanotreatment is often used in lieu of antidepressants. I prescribe it all the time."

"So they have the ability to regulate brain chemistry."

"We think these are programmed to communicate interest in corpo-products and interfere with Serotonin levels. The nightmares might be the result of a lack of exposure to fresh nanoparticles. They don't run forever; they're machines, but the brain can come to rely on them for neurochemical support." She slides her cup over to me, and I refill it.

"Either that, or they're operating on a reward and punishment system."

Halla looks at me over her upraised mug. "We talked about that, too. When I left Yusef at the college, he told me he was going home to wake his family and pack. I doubt he'll ever go back to work."

"Levi was right, then."

"How so?"

"He said some problems were unsolvable and this was one of them." I fold my hands on the table and lean forward. "In the last week, I've interacted with a number of middle-level Peridyne officials, and they don't appear to know what's happening to them. Upper-level officials are part of the corporate infrastructure, so if they know about this, they're facilitating it. And since corpo-villages are privatized, our only recourse would be to contact the state and federal governments."

"Would they believe us?"

"Would it matter? The corpo-villages are mini-states; they have their own, inviolate legal systems and they contribute heavily to election campaigns."

"Unsolvable," she says, and shakes her head.

I lean back and gaze over Halla's shoulder into my study. The desk lamp is on and turned toward my altar, where I had been praying before bed. My wooden statues of Ochosi and Yemaya are illuminated there beside green and blue pillar candles, and a bouquet of spring wildflowers rests between them in a crystal vase.

"Maybe," I answer, "and maybe not."

We are burning sage. It wafts upward through the open casement windows, carrying our prayers to heaven. Wreathed as it is in holy smoke, Maya's basement is a place out of dream. Glass dragons and other beasts hang on fishing twine from a powder-blue ceiling. The walls are painted with murals, mandalas, and little girl musings. Hand-thrown candleholders rise in twisting columns to various heights, illuminating the room in the flickering hues of flame and glass.

My chosen family is here; Maya, Fran, Sammi, Matt, Levi, Dodge, Anni and Sylph. Halla is here too, looking uncomfortable but interested, and I am proud of her for reaching out. There is also a woman I have never met, Sylph's High Priestess from her coven back home, who has come to escort Anni, Maya, Matt and the children to Sunwise Sanctuary at the end of the ritual.

"Please change your mind," Maya's fingers are threaded through mine, and she is looking up at me with wide, haunted eyes. "Come with us."

I put my free hand on her cheek. "I can't. Halla can't do this by herself; she's already addicted, and who knows what else might happen once we expose this?"

Halla is standing behind me, and she circles around to speak to Maya. "I'm sorry we haven't met before, and I'm sorry Adande is involved in this." She wrings her hands. "But I will take care of her and return her to you as soon as I can; I promise."

"Let's get started." Anni moves to the edge of the circle. We link up, and she leads us in a grounding meditation until we are tapped in like the root of an old tree and breathing with the earth beneath our feet. We unlink. She fetches a candle from the altar and walks to the center of the circle.

"The most sacred words a witch can say are 'as I do will, so mote it be'," she begins. "When we say them, we promise to tell the truth always; how can we will anything with mouths that lie? When we say them, we promise to keep our promises; how can we will anything with honor that wavers?"

Halla nods in agreement and relaxes a little. Dodge squeezes her shoulder and smiles encouragement.

Anni continues. "This thing we've discovered is damaging to our will. It makes us want things we don't want. It makes us do things we wouldn't do otherwise. It takes away our most sacred power." She walks clockwise around the circle and looks at each of us in turn. "Tonight we take it back, and tomorrow we start returning it to everyone else."

Sylph joins her in the center of the circle, and together they cleanse it, cast it and bless it. When they're done, Sylph takes the candle from Anni and speaks.

"When you feel ready, come and speak your will to the group."

A moment passes in silence while we all gather our thoughts, pray to our gods, and string the right words together in our minds. Dodge takes the candle first.

"I'm not going anywhere," he says. "I promise to stay right here and watch out for everybody's places while you're gone. It's gonna take more than a bunch of little robots to take _me_ down." He stops, strokes his beard and thinks. Then he approaches the children. "I am a son of the Wolf, and I am your friend. I will walk in your dreams from now until you feel better, and I will guard you. Don't worry if you don't see me; wolves know how to guard from the shadows." He opens his arms and gathers Levi, Fran and Sammi into his embrace. "As I do will, so mote it be."

"So mote it be!" We echo his words, and he passes the candle to me.

"By Libra I come to you," I say as I walk into the circle, "by the Justice card and the balance of scales. I am a woman of Law. I am here to tell you that I will protect your rights and your freedoms, and I will fight until this ugly thing is gone and the people who have done it are punished. By Ochosi and Yemaya I do so swear, and as I do will, so mote it be."

"Yes!" Dodge shouts, clapping his hands.

"So mote it be!" The response is loud and firm; the energy is rising now. Halla reaches for the candle. My eyes widen, but she nods, so I hand it over.

"My name is Halla King-Crichton. I'm a nurse practitioner in Microfield," she says, and steps forward a few paces. "I help people to heal, and I promise to keep doing my job, even if it gets hard. I also promised Maya I would take care of my sister." She looks at me and whispers, "So mote it be?"

"So mote it be!" I say, and grin.

"So mote it be!" The group shouts, and there is more clapping and cheering. Levi walks over to her and asks for the candle. She gives it to him.

"I told Ms. King a couple of days ago that some problems can't be solved." He looks at me and lifts his head. "I'm sorry I said that now. I promise to try and be more hopeful and to help find whatever answers there are."

"I hope that boy marries one of my daughters someday," Maya says, and adds, "I hope his best friend marries the other."

The rite continues. Sylph promises to galvanize her old coven when she gets home. Her High Priestess, an iron-eyed Queen of Swords, promises to network with other sanctuaries and groups so that Pagan refugees have places to go, people to turn to for help. Anni promises to e-mail every warm body in Congress and keep e-mailing them until they start intervening in the matter. Fran and Sammi promise to be good and to help in whatever way they are able.

Matt and Maya take the candle together, and for a moment I wonder if time and separation will turn my beloved's heart in his direction. I feel a spike of jealousy, and then I promise myself that I will love her no matter who she chooses, that I will respect and bless whatever decisions she makes. They approach their children.

"We are your parents," Matt says, his voice shaking, his hands flat against his legs, "and though we don't entirely understand what's happening to you, we _will_ find a way to make things better. So don't worry, okay?"

Maya opens her mouth to speak but begins to cry and falls silent instead. I move forward to put my hands on her waist, and the rest of the circle moves with me. We surround the two families, touch their arms, their heads, and take their hands. We offer solace, compassion and whatever strength our wills can muster.

"So mote it be," Anni says, and puts the candle out.

The coals burn down. We close the circle and file upstairs for food and conversation, passing suitcases, bags and boxes along the way. We don't know when we'll see each other again, so we try a little too hard, laugh a little too loud, and hold our farewells in check until the last possible moment.

"She won't leave you, Aunt Adande," Sammi finds me alone on the porch, struggling to compose myself so that I can go back to the party. She reaches up, takes my hand and pulls me down to eye level. Her gray eyes are clear and deep, and her long hair is pulled back into two tight braids.

"You don't think so?" I ask her, and wonder how old her soul is.

"She loves you, and so do we. We don't leave the people we love just because we're apart for a while."

Old, I decide. Very old indeed. I stand up, and we go back into the house together.

A Path Without Bones

How do we journey on a path without bones,
far away from the place where our ancestors lie,
when the coins of tradition are not ours to spend,
and the mounds of sweet poetry not ours to tend?

Lend me a staff, Gods, and show me the way.

How do we pray on this alien wind,
far away from the place where our people drew breath,
when the jargon of penitence fills up our lungs,
and we speak with mouths opened by conquering
    tongues?

Lend me a tale, Gods, and teach me to sing.

How do we live disconnected from home,
far away from the wisdom they left on the land,
when the soil of our bodies belongs to this place,
and the ground of our being has found a new face?

Lend me a stone, Gods, and help me to build.

Two Servants of the Morrighan

When She led the army at Maigh Tuireadh, She had a
    legitimate foe.
Your bad tattoos, your stint with cocaine, your failure to
    thrive are your fault.
I don't care what you're calling yourself now.

Didn't you get the memo? Queens don't need to play the
    twenty-something cunt -
or spit epithets at the backs of Christian colleagues to
    bring change,
not especially Queens who can dance on the point of a
    spear.

She came to me huge and black and seething with
    maggots when I was your age.
*"Die to yourself. Be reborn in yourself. Let the infection be
    cleansed."*
I was slick and sleek and shining after the flies hatched.

And when I sounded her depth at Emhain Macha, She
    spoke sooth behind my teeth,
but She neglected to mention whether or not you should
    go back to waitressing after grad school -
because you hate this shit and everybody here.

She did say the sons of Ulster are still at war with one
    another,
and their birth pangs are the sorrow of nations.
Have you ever prayed for their release? Do you even
    know why Conchobhar's men were cursed?

She doesn't exist to grant us permission, and we are the
    least of Her concerns.
"Keep the pace or step aside. Do the work or pass the tools.
    Speak the truth or shut up."
Whose blood do you think the Badb wrings from our
    clothes?

Yundah

- *Yundah*: A sealwoman chant from the Outer Hebrides. (Scottish)
- *Yundah*: An expression that explains the value of exchange through trading. (Australian Aboriginal)

KAT DUG these graves for me six months before she passed away. She was waning fast, but she got up one morning in a final fit of vigor and made sure that every living thing in our care had a place to go when it died. I put her in the wheelbarrow when the cancer took her; she wanted to crawl out to it the night before so I wouldn't have to move her body, but I held her close to my breasts and whispered our best stories into her ears until she fell asleep listening to them. It took me six hours to get her here, and Fergus followed me all the way, his old black tail beating against my leg. Now and again he'd whine and bury his snout in my sweater, and I would put the wheelbarrow down and grieve with him, for Kat, for the way it was ending, for the dog-sized hole he would fill someday soon. That was two years ago.

The only old dog at the gravesite today is me, and the weather is upon me now, real and true. This autumn Samhain came in like a late summer storm; it blew still-blooming petals off asters too confused to know they should be dying. Fergus laid on the couch and watched their fat little yellow and white heads bend in the wind through a window that shouldn't have been open that late in the season. I'm sure he thought it was a good thing; the sunlight warmed his bones, and the wind gave his doggy nose something to do. But I could hear the earth under my feet, under the floor, through the concrete in the basement, and I knew the asters were right to feel disoriented.

We saw it coming, Kat and I. I was twenty-four when the hurricanes first hit Florida, but even then my Mother was strong in me, so I could tell it was the beginning of an Age. Kat said it wouldn't be too long before the U.S. started folding northward into itself; its southern cities abandoned to the heat, the high water, the insects, and the poor. I imagined a mass migration like a great tsunami rolling up through Atlanta, Boston, Portland, and eventually into Toronto and Montreal, destroying everything in its wake.

"Megan, we have to get settled and get busy," Kat said to me the weekend my grandmother died. My chest tightened a little when she said it; it was hard to think of grandma in the past tense. But she was right. The house and orchard were mine now, and if we were going to survive long enough to be old women ourselves, we had to start making use of the gift soon. So she quit school, I left my job at the hospital, and we drove all the way east until we came to my grandparents' apple orchard gracing the shoreline and their old, white, maritime farmhouse standing sentinel on a hillside overlooking the waves.

Nova Scotia was good for my Kat. She was a McElroy on her mother's side, a fire maiden by birth sign and by complexion, and she had always wanted to walk in the way of her ancestors. She signed up for Gàidhlig classes at the Cape Breton college the day we unpacked the moving van. Of course, she didn't tell anybody up there that she was a Pagan. But she brought the language home with her in little packets of verbal joy and spiced the Eco-Scottish soup of our rituals with things she learned during her weekends away.

On the first full moon after we arrived, we blessed the place. I'd already done so many times before while grandma was alive, but this time it was my land to care for; I could feel it in the stroke of my axe on the deadwood in the orchard and smell it in the water when the tide was in. Kat brought her first Gàidhlig to the ceremony and taught me to say "tha seo math" instead of "so mote it be" at the end. After that we called many things good, and there was a lot of good to call.

Kelsey, Grace, and Jared moved into the apartment above the garage five years later. A few months after that, Hannah was born. It had been hard for them to explain to their families how important they were to one another, especially after Grace, the only one of them who wasn't a legal part of the marriage, conceived a child. Jared's father had been a commercial lobsterman and a big man in Downeast Maine, so there was a lot of backlash, and they stood to lose their home over it when collective cruelty of their neighbors reached critical mass. Kat met them at a class in Cape Breton, and after they danced around the subject of spirituality long enough to realize they were dancing to the same tune, they became friends. When she found out about their predicament, she brought them home like stray kittens and asked me if they could stay.

I knew the orchard and garden would bloom earlier that year than it had in years past, and I knew they would never bloom late again in my lifetime. I knew we would have to start planting more, harvesting more, and preserving more if we expected to be independent. We would need the extra hands to keep up with it all, but it was hard for me to say yes.

"I'm worried I might need them," Kat confessed to me that night after she tucked them into the guest beds and found me down at the shoreline again, scrubbing my naked arms and legs with handfuls of cold, wet sand. "You're so connected...you journey to places where I can't follow. What would happen if you went out one day and never came all the way back? How would I care for you and this place all by myself?"

"There isn't anything wrong with me; I just can't seem to get clean in the house." I looked into her eyes, so dark in the moonlight, and prayed I would find understanding there. It was early March, but the snow was already melting, and I could hear the earth awake and angry under my feet, like an eight-to-fiver jolted out of bed at 5:00 a.m. by a passing siren. "The water in the house feels like the soil in the orchard, but the ocean doesn't care yet. It's easier here."

"Is that why you wanted to drill another well farther inland? Why you have trouble drinking the water here?"

"No, we might really need that extra well someday...and yes." My hands had begun to shake in the cold, but I gathered up another handful of sand and kept working.

She smiled, reached out from beneath her knitted wrap, and put her hand on my cheek. "You know, I half expect to find your sealskin locked in some barnacle-encrusted trunk on the shoreline someday, waiting there for me to die so that you can climb back into it and return to the water where you belong." She took my hair in her hands, a tangled mess of black curls, and braided it with nimble fingers until it was out of her way. "My ancestors sang about women like you." And then she was scrubbing my back and hips with broad, quick strokes, warming the sand and my skin with her touch.

There was a red tide bloom in May the year Hannah started

keeping bees, and a few days later our little beach was smothered in rotting cod. It took a long time clear them away, but I'd sensed the algae growing in the water a week before we found the fish and brought gloves and buckets down to the water line in a plastic, 50-gallon drum. The next day, I drove into town and brought back twenty chestnut saplings. By the time we had a use for the gloves and buckets, the trees were already in the ground. It would be the better part of a decade before they began to produce enough to supplement the protein we derived from sea life, but Jared believed he could keep us in fish for awhile yet, especially if I could tell him when a bloom was imminent.

And I could. The days had long since passed when I allowed my connection to upset me. In truth, I'd begun to believe all living things possessed the same bond with the earth to some degree or another, and I came to wonder why nobody else I'd met heard and saw and felt what I did. As for me, I knew when to prune the orchard now by the keening of branches in the wind. I could hear the voice of the clouds herald the onset of bad weather several days before it actually arrived, so we almost never lost a harvest or a hive. It was like a drum in my soul, this consciousness; on the upbeat, I knew a thing was coming and made ready to receive it; on the downbeat, the thing came, and my instrument rested awhile. And when my Mother was sure I knew the rhythm to her satisfaction, she sent me farther afield to places where orphaned coyote pups needed food, or raspberries needed seeding, or trees needed planting. Sometimes I was gone for days, but I always managed to get back in time to keep us from harm.

On one such occasion I returned to find a very pregnant Kelsey teaching Hannah to milk goats I'd never seen before. Hannah spied me coming up the gravel road and came running, her dwindling girlishness outweighing her pre-teen desire for personal space, and threw herself into my arms.

"Aunt Megan, we have goats! And one of them is going to have a kid!"

"You shouldn't talk about your mother that way."

"I heard that," Kelsey shouted up the road at me as she tied her sun-bleached hair into a knot and then rested her brown arms on her belly. She was glorious, a happy woman finally pregnant after years of trying, and she would be dead within the week. I was so confident, certain I could handle so natural a thing as bringing a child into the world after four years of nursing school and more than fifteen years at my Mother's knee that when I felt the upbeat of a massive postpartum hemorrhage, I dismissed it as the work of a hyperactive imagination. My Mother wouldn't do that to me. The downbeat took Kelsey away from us.

Grace named the boy Logan and spent the rest of her life in the shadow of Jared's legal wife's ghost. Jared walled Kelsey's memory up in a room of pain with no doors and threw himself at Grace with a fervor that bordered on frenzy. I laid my ear to the drum and never got up again, not even when I was filthy and malnourished and frostbitten, not even when my fire maiden bathed me, fed me, and wept over my wounds.

Only Kat survived somewhat whole. She and Hannah started working climate magic together when Hannah failed to come out of that cave of quiet where grieving girls go. Over time she emerged though, a weather witch in her own right, come of age in an era when weather wasn't what it used to be and needed all the help it could get. A regular circle came of that work, and Pagans from all over the province brought their wills to bear on the changing planet thirteen times a year for many years, while I went through menopause and empathized with the problems intrinsic to permanent change.

It was the chalcid wasps that finally brought me some measure of peace. The winter after Logan turned twenty-three, there wasn't enough frost kill to keep the bacteria and the bugs from destroying the orchards when the weather warmed. We fought all spring to keep a fire blight down only to be hit with aphids and apple maggots in the heat of summer, when it was hardest to work during the daytime. I couldn't imagine what was happening farther south; the bugs and the heat nearly killed us. But just when we thought we had lost the orchards entirely, the wasp larvae got their wings and descended on the trees like a squadron of attack bombers, glistening and deadly. I watched for three days while they harvested the parasites out of our way and Logan built the smokers that would chase them off before they turned from the bugs to the fruit. His hands were strong and calloused; but his hair was like his mother's, and he tied it up when he went to work with a grace so like hers that it broke my heart to watch him. Everything living wants to live, but nothing lives forever.

We found six people in the chestnut orchard in late August of that same year. They were gathering nuts into burlap bags they must have taken from our barn in the night. We thought they had probably slept there too, since the goats didn't need milking that morning when Hannah went out to them. So Jared and Logan loaded their rifles and went out looking for what they thought were thieves. What they found was a wake-up call.

"Please, let us work. We just want to work," a youngish man with a weathered, brown face pleaded with them from behind a half-full bag. "We were hungry and tired last night, but we didn't want to take anything from you without giving something back." An older woman who might have been his mother put her hand on his shoulder and hefted her bag in Logan's direction.

"We'll do whatever you ask," she said. "This just looked like it needed doing, so I put these people to work early. We thought it best to show you some good faith."

"What are you doing here?" Jared asked them, and lowered his gun. "Where are you from?"

"I'm from Bangor," said a plump, brown haired woman of about thirty.

"Woodstock."

"Moncton."

"The three of us are from Boston," the mother offered, and pointed to another youngish man in the group. "We've been traveling together for some time now."

"Why?" Logan asked, puzzled.

"You don't get out much, do you?" said the first man. "The U.S. and Canadian border is closed, has been since midsummer. We've met a lot of people like us, going north to where the food is. If you need anything from what's left of civilization, I suggest you get it soon. There aren't many delivery trucks on the roads since the border closed, and there isn't as much to buy anymore."

So Hannah, Grace, and I took the trailer into town, drew every dime out of the farm's account, and went shopping. We bought bolts of cloth, thread, and needles. We updated our tool kit, our cookware, our linens, and our first aid supplies. We picked up lamp and candle wicks, lamp oil, fuel by the five-gallon drum and the equipment to manufacture a distillery. Finally, we stocked up on as many supplies for the windmill, the solar panels, the fences, the roofs, and the plumbing as our remaining money would allow. On the way home, Grace said that it was a good day. Hannah called it a day of severance.

Logan left with the work crew three weeks later. How could we have kept him? He was young, he had never been to public school, never seen much of anything beyond his home, and he had a right to live, despite the times. Grace and Jared blamed themselves and blamed their enduring grief, but to their credit, they never let Logan see it. We made him promise to come home if ever he was hungry or in trouble. We gave him a first aid kit, a set of cookware, and one of our precious rifles. We released him to the world. He said he'd be back the next spring to help with the pruning and planting, but we never saw him again.

That autumn and winter were the deadliest I'd ever seen. Storm surges battered the orchard closest to the shoreline so often and so hard I knew it would never recover, so I took the gas-powered chainsaw out to the trees we had just worked so hard to save and used a measure of our dwindling gasoline to cut them all down before the ocean bore them away. They had fed my family for four generations; my whole childhood was tangled up in their branches, and I owed them a proper funeral. So I got up every morning for two weeks before breakfast and went out to them in the wind, in the ice, in the high tides and keened over each one as I butchered and dismembered it for its hot-burning wood. When Jared came out to help me, I sent him away. When Hannah came out to reason with me, I sent her away too. Only Kat got close enough to bring me hot food and to put fragrant, homemade salve on my face and hands. My work gloves still smell of it after all these years, if I bury my face in them and breathe deep.

And then a bizarre, late-season hurricane made landfall and ripped the roof right off the barn, leaving the chickens, the goats, and our dried foods exposed to the weather until we could get everything into the house and garage. We lost so much of our winter stores that I was almost glad Logan had gone away; I wasn't sure we could feed five people, four goats, a flock of chickens and a dog on what we had left. As it turned out, we didn't feed many of the animals that hard, hard season; they fed us.

The following spring, most of the wildlife left the coast, with the exception of a few brave creatures that lived on whatever they could find locally. Our neighbors went with them, so there was no reason to go into town anymore; nobody was there. And Kat's weather-working circle, a staple of the local Pagan community for over twenty years, dwindled away until only she and Hannah and Fergus were left to call the quarters and pray.

I didn't leave the property all that summer; I felt my Mother's need all right, but it was always close by, and I was always busy. The chestnuts continued to produce, and the apple trees I planted near the second well offered up a respectable crop despite the drought, but I couldn't keep up with the orchards, the increasing vagaries of red tide bloom that required so much precision of spirit to predict, and the sickly animals orphaned by rail-thin mothers who went out for breakfast and never came back. I couldn't hold it all together anymore and still maintain the soul wall that allowed me to keep drinking our well water and eating our food without vomiting up the riotous earth out of my stomach. I was getting old.

Late in July, Hannah made it official. "Mom and dad want to go inland, but they're afraid to tell you so. You've been so good to them, to all of us, but they don't want to grow old in a place they can't maintain, a place where they might not have access to hospitals or doctors when they become frail." She paused, and gathering her strength added, "We should all go together."

"There might not be any place for us to settle inland," Kat told her as she bundled comfrey and strung it along the kitchen crossbeam. "And what about Logan? Don't you want to wait for him?"

"I don't think Logan is coming back." Her voice was soft and strained, and she looked out of the kitchen window and down the gravel road to the place where it met the tree line. "I was all he ever had, and he was all I ever had, so one of us had to go, and he wanted me to take care of our parents." She swallowed hard and looked back into Kat's eyes. They widened for a moment while the fine lines around her mouth deepened into a frown and her brow furrowed in thought. Then she nodded once, briskly, and turned to me.

"I can't leave; you know that," I told her. "But you could." She had been pale these last few months, and she tired more easily than she used to. She insisted she was just getting old herself, but my ear was still fixed to the drum, and I knew a thing was coming. I wanted more than anything to be two women that day; to go with my beloved into whatever safety Hannah hoped she could find for us and to stay here, where my Mother still spoke to me in angry whispers from behind the fragments of that wall in my soul.

Kat pulled the wooden combs out of her red and silver hair and refitted them snugly. "You won't get rid of me that easily my love, so put your skin back in the trunk and quit dreaming of the sea. It'll be there for you soon enough, when you're ready for it."

"Go tell your parents to come up to the house." I took Hannah by the shoulders and kissed her cheek while she looked from me to Kat, bemused. "I'll make some tea."

We gave them the truck and trailer; it was theirs as much as ours, and Jared had done a lot of fine work installing the solar panels and converting the fuel system. They laid out a trip plan; Halifax, Fredericton, and then up into Schefferville. They asked us to give it to Logan if he returned, and we promised we would. And then they stammered their love and their sorrow at us and begged us to come with them, even though we all could sense it was time for us to go our separate ways.

It was easier than I thought it would be to let Grace and Jared go; we had been friends, family for the better part of four decades, but I had long ago lost my taste for people and the fuel they needed to stay alive and the dung they left behind. Hannah was a different story though, she was like my own child. When I saw that she had become so hollow she echoed herself when she talked, I took her for a walk in the chestnuts.

"It was wrong of us to keep the two of you here so long," I told her, and she finally wept.

"We never made love. We never even came close. But there was always this tension between us...we used to lie in each other's arms and cry. I loved him so much."

"Do your parents know?"

"I don't think so." She wiped her face on her shirt and smoothed it back into place. "You couldn't have cared for us better if you tried, Aunt Megan. This wasn't your fault. It wasn't anybody's fault."

"It was everybody's fault. It still is." I took her in my arms and cried with her awhile. "Go find somebody to love you. You've done all you can, too."

And then they were gone. Kat and I spent the rest of the season converting the lower level of the garage into living space for the goats and the upper level into a kind of apothecary where Kat would have plenty of room to dry herbs and make medicines. The barn had never completely recovered from last year's weather; we just couldn't spare the supplies to make good repairs. So before the hurricane season began, I took a shoulder bag of things we had made with Kat's herbs and Hannah's honey and walked inland to the First Nations reservation, hoping to set up some sort of trade with whoever was left there.

"We have our own bees," I was told when I arrived, and I heard an accusation in the tone that I thought was at odds with the rusted-out cars and empty casinos around them. So I went home, and we made do with what we had in the time we had left.

It was cervical cancer, and it came on slow. Kat waned like a moon, over time, bright until she was gone. It took almost five years. In that time we saw the shoreline move inland and storm surges edge toward the chestnut trees. I was always a step ahead of it though, quick in my soul to compensate for my slow body. Our luck held us through those final seasons; the hurricanes took a little of the barn away each time they passed over, but the house and garage held on, tenacious and loyal.

By the time Kat took the shovel out to the woods, we both knew what was coming, just like we had known in the beginning. I couldn't help her dig that day; my ankle was injured and swollen. We were both afraid it might be a fracture. So I hobbled out on handmade crutches and tried not to think about the reasons I hadn't already done what she was about to do.

"You'll be heading back to the ocean soon," she said, leaning against a tree, surveying her work. There were five deep ditches in the grove, two for the goats, one for Fergus, and one more, human-sized.

"And where will you go?" I asked her, and laid my hand on her knee and my forehead on her thigh.

"Into the ground, and into the grove, and into your soul," she said, and put her hand on my head.

"Oh Kat, I am so tired."

"I know," she said. She had always known.

On the way up to Kat's grave this morning I was thinking about that trip to the reservation. I guess I don't blame those people for being wary of me; I don't even blame them for blaming me, if that's what they were doing at all. There's plenty of blame to go around, and I do think they saw it coming before I did. But wasn't I worthy too? Didn't I stain my hands in the soil and listen to the voices of the earthworms that turned it? Didn't I leave a measure of my harvest on the ground every year for the squirrels and raccoons and deer brave enough to remain here with us? Didn't I answer the rain when it asked me to explain its frenzied passage across the sky, and didn't I weep with it over the orphans I couldn't save? Didn't I go down to the ocean at red tide and lay hands on the crooked little corpses of my Mother's children and answer for the crime that brought them there?

I found seaweed in the orchard again last week. The tide was high, higher than it has ever been, and I know there won't be any chestnuts next year. So I've put the letter from Logan's family on

68

the kitchen table along with a list of things that ought to be done throughout the year and when he ought to do them, just in case. I don't think there's anything else I can do here; I've given what I had to give, and I've received what my Mother could offer me in trade. It was a good bargain. When the tide comes back again, I intend to ebb with it, as Fergus ebbed, as Kat ebbed, as we all must. From the sea we come, and to the sea do we return, to come from the sea again. If we are careful.

Tha seo math.

Mine Is the Night Ocean

Mine is the night ocean,
the fog ocean,
the wild ocean.

Here the implacable sea prays, herself to herself,
in the stone-crushing crackle of undertow.
Here the brine foam sings of salted lungs -
and the fish that pick flesh clean.

Lulled, leaning in, arms wide as a heron's wings
tidal gravity luring me on to the water's edge,
the pitch of my body like ship tilting leeward,
the drum of the surf rumbling in my bones -

I know fear, and the conquering of it, and I am cleansed.

Mine is the night ocean,
the fog ocean,
the wild ocean.

Bringing Woden to the Little Green Men

Fame unto Woden, fierce folk-compass,
surveyor of vastness for valorous travelers,
that we might wander to worlds uncharted,
deciphering sooth with star-dwellers.

Lo. A loyal soul, a liegeman of Woden,
priest of the people was Pieter Heinle.
Clever and crafty, he came to a planet -
that rolled around a ruby sun.
Small folk he found there, frondy and verdant,
bold, bright-faced beacons of life.
They greeted him warmly, giving him gifts.
Their reception of strangers was song-worthy.

Then, Hávamál in hand, he hoisted his arm -
and read of the runes, right-finding way-guides.
The crowd was transfixed, few were afraid,
but no one was wise to the word-way he used.
When he concluded, they cooed, curled up,

and spat on each other, singing and swaying.
So he could not ken them; cleverness failed him.
Those vegetables vexed the Valfather's son.

Yet he wot he could win them without language.
Charades and relics render meaning as well.
So night fell to morning, and he met them mounted -
on a statue of Sleipnir, a wooden stallion,
and galloped through gardens, green nurseries,
where petaled plant-babies peered up from the brush.
He grew weary thus, so he gathered the group -
to drink from the mead horn while he made mighty oaths.
But alas! Liquor left them unwell;
their fronds blackened, and a few of them fainted.

Pieter was moved to pause and ponder -
the hubris of holy work among the wholly alien.
His message was muddled, many were ill,
and he had not come to cause chaos.
So he chose sacrifice instead of ceremony,
the wail of Woden upon the World Ash,
and hung himself high, head inverted -
on a bending branch bristling with needles.

He fell in a faint, but the tree fed him,
piercing his flesh and pushing in painlessly,
knotting, nesting near his marrow.
His head lolled; his lips loosened.
The tongue of the tree twined with Pieter's,
and runes flushed, flowered, fell from his mouth.
The crowd caught them, came to ken them,
and spat on the priest, who sang and swayed -
with the bending branch, above the people.

Some say he swings in that garden, still.

So fame unto Woden, fierce folk-compass,
surveyor of vastness for valorous travelers,
that we might wander to worlds uncharted,
deciphering sooth with star-dwellers.

The Ruin of Beltany Ring

No ONE CAME to pray at the Beltany ring anymore. Even the stains left behind by bleeding women and their flowers had been weathered away so long that none of the peering scientists who used to visit could tell for what purpose the cup-marked stones were fashioned. The peering scientists did not come anymore either, and the young people who did left their saliva and their sperm and their condoms behind, an ill-dignified offering where once the fluid energy of life was food for the circle, the land it graced and food that was harvested from it. The only regular visitors now were the wind that howled around the pillars and the ravens that flew in on their way to somewhere else, all newsy and full of their own lives.

And so the stones began to talk to one another in the slow, creaking cadence of stone speech. They had heard about Long Meg and her Daughters from a murder of ravens who had recently nested in Cumberland, wherever that was. One day the rocks lifted their skirts and fled to the ocean, flinging themselves at the waves in a fit of despair. The ravens had also told them the Carrowkeel Passage Cemetery had opened its depths to tourists, and now the deep under-Ireland was regularly invaded by picture-happy treasure-hunters in search of leprechauns. Shameful. It was rumored as well that the Daghda was holding court at Grianan Ailigh and fertilizing barren women to sold-out crowds. One would hope the stones of that place would fall upon his head before they allowed such things to happen.

This conversation went on for some time; it was a complaint really, like some people complain about the weather. Suicide was not an option; they would not go the way of Long Meg. Too many sweet-faced girls had pressed their warm, round bellies against the limestone and begged for ten fingers and ten toes and strong lungs. And there would be no talk of meaty-fisted tourists or freak shows either; too many grandmothers had surrendered their last praying for the children those sweet-faced girls brought into the world. But sometimes the wind keened just so, and sometimes the ravens were so cruel, chatting on and on about cathedrals in Paris, wherever that was, and the women who carried flowers into them day and night. It had been too long, even as stones measure time, since people had come into the circle with reverence in their hearts.

Until one day, some time after the conversation began, a woman came alone, not the wind, not a raven, not a rutting couple and their rubbish, and prayed. Her belly was not big, there were no lines on her face, and she made no offering. She didn't even look like the women who used to come; her skin was the color freshly-turned soil, and her eyes were like the spaces between the stars. But her voice was stretched, and her eyes were wet, and the stones remembered these signs. So they settled into stillness and listened while she walked between and among them, her warm, sturdy hands flaking away the centuries as she stroked their weathered surfaces.

"I am so stupid," she whispered after a time as she sat against the cup-marked stone in the northeast, her face upturned to catch the sunlight. "You are a clock of some kind, and that is all you are. I was wrong to come here, to hope for help, to remember a thing that never happened. This was just a story I told myself a long time ago when I was lonely and needed someplace to call home." The woman paused and inhaled a long, shuddering breath. "But it was a good story, and I'm not sorry I told it, even if you are just a clock."

Then the woman did a strange thing. She got up on her knees, lifted her sweater and laid her smooth, flat belly on the front of the stone. For a long time, she looked out over the Dhún na nGall hills while the sun crept across them, leaving shadows in its wake. And then, when the shadows were wider than the sunlight, she turned her face to the earth, wrapped her arms around the triangular top of the stone and bathed it in her tears. After a time the sun set, the moon rose, and the woman went away in sorrow.

And in sorrow, the stone drank her tears to discern the place of her origin, but the salt of the woman's body was unfamiliar to it. So it asked the ravens, who had watched the whole affair with great interest, if they had ever seen her before. But the ravens were cagey and mean, and it took a great deal of flattery to get anything useful out of them. In the end, they confessed no knowledge of the woman but said they had seen others like her.

"The Hurlers and the Girdle Stanes say there are people like her who come to them all the time and make odd prayers; they sit against the stones and cry. Then they go away and never come back. Who knows who they are? Who cares?"

This was a thing of considerable interest to the Beltany ring, and the circle fairly swayed with excitement. So when the wind keened around the pillars, they didn't hear it, and when the ravens changed the subject to flowers and cathedrals and Prague, wherever that was, they didn't listen. Here, they saw, was the path away from despair, away from sacrilege, away from the condoms and rubbish. But were they strong enough to part the veil and bring to bear the grace they had been given so long ago? Had the blood and the flowers faded out of them entirely? Was there no essence left, deep in the rock, where only they could see it? And how would they know where to find these people and their odd prayers, and how would the people receive them?

This quarrelsome rumbling and crunching of boulder against boulder went on for many days until the triangular, cup-marked stone remembered the woman's tears, counted their salt against its strength and began, itself, to pray. Back and back it prayed, beyond the visit of the soil-skinned woman, past the centuries of dwindling interest and rising thoughtlessness, deep into the company of the women who loved the Beltany ring best. It had no way of knowing whether or not these girls and mothers and grandmothers understood its need, but it asked for their blessings anyway. So while they touched a new cup-marked stone with their hands and their bellies and their breasts and their blood and their flowers, an old cup-marked stone touched them back with its sorrow and the sorrow of a night-eyed supplicant.

When it returned across the sunlight and shadow of the Dhún na nGall hillside, its voice was the stone upon stone of a great door opening, and its companions were amazed at what they heard. But one by one, around the circle sunwise, they echoed the sound. And the sun set, and the moon rose, and the Beltany stones winked out of sight altogether.

When they winked back into sight, Dhún na nGall was gone. In its place, a long string of mountains stretched north and south and into the heavens. It was early evening; the sun was an orange quarter-disk in the western sky, and they could hear a murder of startled crows speeding off in the direction of the darkness. The stones exhaled, and their voices fell into silence.

Out of that silence came the thump of a drum and the sound of laughter from a nearby hillside where a circle of dancing people were threading bright ribbons around a tall pole sunk deep into the ground. A moment later the drum paused, and the laughter fell into silence. An instant passed. An age passed. And out of that silence came the ee-ya-ha cry of a soil-skinned, night-eyed woman, the rustling of garments, and the thunder of twenty-six feet running down from the hillside and into the Beltany ring, weeping, cheering, and singing praises.

It was many hours before the pillars realized the triangular, cup-marked stone was missing from the northeast. By then, the rest of the ring was covered in ribbons and candles and half-eaten food and half-drunk wine. The women and men and children and all their odd prayers were sleeping on the grass, under the stars, in the center of the circle, and the night-eyed woman sat in the place of the missing stone, naked from the waist up. Her arms were wrapped around her softening belly, and her face shone. If the stones could have wept with joy, they would have. But instead, they contented themselves with the whisper of the night breeze, the hooting of owls, and the clutter of reverent strangers.

And so there is a single, cup-marked stone in County Dhún na nGall where the Beltany ring used to stand, a stone that knows how to open a door and how to close it again, a stone that knows when to begin a prayer and when to end it. The wind still howls around this stone, and the ravens still chatter down at it, but the bellies and the tears and the prayers of countless women shield it, too. From time to time, when it is especially lonely, it prays to those women. And from time to time, when they are especially strong, they respond.

Godtouched

Some days You are nearer than my skin,
so near I can feel my small hand in Your great one,
and Your voice, like music, pulses over my eardrums.

Some days we breathe, like lungs, together,
and You saturate my mind like a river of honey -
over a crust of bread, so unbearably sweet.

Some days this barrier between the seen and the unseen -
aches like a wound, so great is the pressure upon the veil,
and we meet, as if on opposite sides of a window -

Touching our fingers to the pane,
and waiting for the glass to warm.

Bibliography

MacCath, C.S. 2010. "Fetters." *Goblin Fruit*, January 2010.

McCath-Moran, C.S. 2004. "Ink for the Dead." *NewWitch*, December 2004.

MacCath, C.S. 2011. "When I Arrived, This Is What She Said." *Goblin Fruit*, October 2011.

MacCath, C.S. 2006. "Ηφαιστος." *Illumen*, October 2006.

McCath, C.S. 2006. "Ammonite Baby." *NewWitch*, May 2006.

MacCath, C.S. 2006. "Στεφανοσ." *Mythic Delirium*, May 2006.

MacCath, C.S. 2010. "The Interstitial Fairy Demolition Crew Casts a Circle." *Eternal Haunted Summer*, 20 June 2010.

MacCath, C.S. 2008. "From Our Minds to Yours." In *The Pagan Anthology of Short Fiction: 13 Prize Winning Tales*, edited by Anne Newkirk Niven and Diana Paxson, 87–104. Woodbury: Llewellyn Worldwide.

MacCath, C.S. 2010. "A Path Without Bones." *Eternal Haunted Summer*, March 2010.MacCath, C.S. 2007. "Two Servants of the Morrighan." *Mythic Delirium*, June 2007.

MacCath, C.S. 2005. "Yundah." *PanGaia*, December 2005.

MacCath, C.S. 2008. "Bringing Woden to the Little Green Men." *PanGaia*, January 2008.

MacCath, C.S. 2009. "The Ruin of Beltany Ring." *Witches & Pagans*, September 2009.

MacCath, C.S. 2009. "Godtouched." *Witches & Pagans*, September 2009.